To Douglas, my husband, best friend, life partner and soulmate -- whose love and acceptance allows me the freedom to continue to grow, change and "become" who I am meant to be. Our life together is one incredible adventure after another. Thanks for being my co-pilot on this journey.

To my parents, Barbara and Will -- whose belief in me and constant love and support through the many paths of my life gives me the strength and courage to continue to take on new challenges. I believed you when you told me, as a little girl, that I could be anything I wanted. (I'm still deciding...)

To all my friends and family -- who have been my personal cheering squad, thanks for helping me through this interesting transition from attorney to author.

I love you all, Rainey

Published by:
DreamDog Press
3686 King Street, Suite 160
Alexandria, Virginia 22302

To Order...Toll-Free
1-877-2-RAINEY
1-877-272-4639

www.dreamdog.com

Copyright © 1999 by Lorraine Friedman
Illustrated by Betsy Dill
Production and layout by Doug Hamann

Publisher's Cataloging-in-Publication
(Provided by Quality Books, Inc.)

Friedman, Lorraine Lee.
Monsters in your bed-- monsters in your head / by Rainey ; illustrated by Betsy Dill. -- 1st ed.
p. cm.
SUMMARY: Angie is frightened by the monsters she imagines in her bedroom at night, until her magical dog Jazz empowers her by teaching her to name each one, say good-bye to it, and help it find a home of its own.
LCCN: 98-93647
ISBN: 0-9666199-1-9

1. Fear of the dark--Juvenile fiction. 2. Dogs--Juvenile fiction. 3. Monsters--Juvenile fiction. I. Dill, Betsy. II. Title.

PZ8.3.F91155Mo 1999   [E]
                    QB198-1522

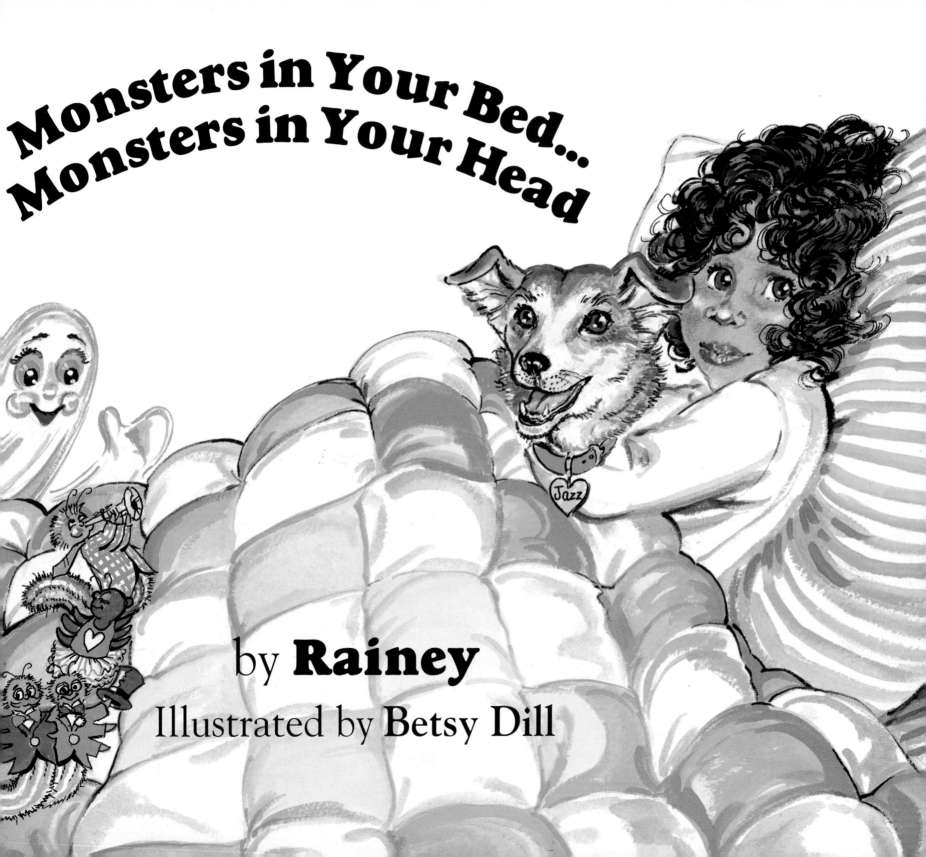

Monsters in Your Bed...
Monsters in Your Head

by **Rainey**

Illustrated by Betsy Dill

Tucked in her bed, late at night,
Angie couldn't sleep without the light.
She feared the dark would bring out creatures,
but dared not think about their features.

She imagined a dragon with heads at both ends
and spikes in the middle where he begins.

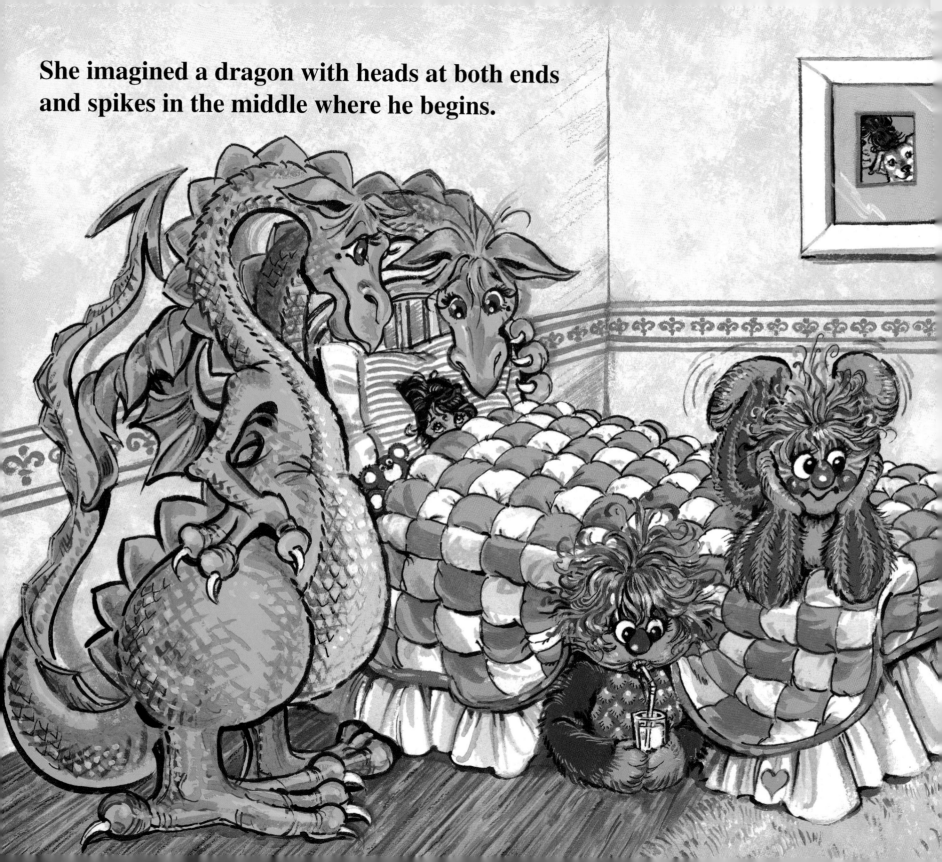

Angie saw monsters of purple and blue
and shuddered to think what they might do.

The caterpillars of orange and red
she imagined would come in and dance on her head.

And the silvery snake that climbed on the wall
was, to Angie, the most frightening of all.

He slithered and swayed this way and that,
coming dangerously close to touching a bat.

The bats were yellow with spots of green,
and Angie thought they looked rather mean.

She pulled the covers up over her head
and shivered in her little bed.

She peeked out and heard the ghosts call
as they floated about, outside in the hall.

Each night was the same; she imagined them coming and couldn't stop the noises from humming.

She called her dog Jazz and held her so tight;
she thought this might help her let go of the fright.

So Jazz stood watch at the foot of the bed,
and between her two paws, she rested her head.

She sniffed and she growled into the air
but was quite sure that nothing was there.

Then, Jazz had an idea and to Angie she said:
"I think that these monsters are all in your head.
I've listened for signals and looked for a sign,
but I think that these creatures are just in your mind.

So let's say good night and sweet dreams to your friends
and hope that by doing so your fantasy ends."
Angie was still shaking, but thought it worth a try.
In the tiniest little voice, she said: "good-bye."

"No... one at a time, you have to address them by name,
then we can say good-bye to your scary night game."

Holding Jazz tightly, she started with the dragon,
who she noticed was sitting in her little red wagon.

"Good night Mr. Dragon, with a head at both ends;
I think you'd be more comfortable in one of the dens.
There are pillows and cushions and a whole lot more room,
but I'm sending the others so you better zoom."

And as the words floated into the air,
she looked at the wagon and the dragon wasn't there.
"They're gone," whispered Angie still in awe,
shaking the DreamDog by her paw.

"Hmm," thought Jazz, "that must be it.
The reason the haunting and moaning won't quit.
Those monsters you see have no place to roam...
all that they need is their very own home.

And you found them a new place to live;
that was the best gift you could possibly give."
So, Angie thought about it for a little while
as her lips turned up in an all-knowing smile.

Then, on to the monsters of purple and blue,
and this time Angie knew just what to do.
"Sweet dreams, monsters, but you can't sleep in here.
There's not enough room... that much is clear.

I think you'd be happier in an open space,
and I happen to know just the right place.

There's an old mill, shut down for quite some time;
I think that you'd like all the grit and the grime."
And the monsters nodded saying "thanks" on their way
and headed to the mill to scare and to play.

"Good night caterpillars," Angie said with a giggle,
"you need to go outside where there's more room to wiggle.
In my backyard, there are flowers and trees.
You could make new friends with all the bugs and the bees."

**And the caterpillars waved all their hands and feet
and boogied on out to their own special beat.**

Then she heard a hiss from the silvery snake,
the same noise that used to make Angie shake.
But, she waved good-bye and blew him a kiss
and said to herself, "Oh, I can do this!"

"Hey little snake, you should be outside on the ground;
in the warm mud you can slither around."

And, just like that no more snake — now the bats,
who were trying on mittens, mufflers and hats.

"Good night, yellow bats with spots of green;
time for you to leave this scene.
You must be too cold," Angie started to rave;
"why not go find a warm dark cave?"

And the bats flew out of the room into the night,
and now there were no more creatures in sight.
Then she heard the 'woo-wooing' out in the hall
and bravely said, "come on in here you all."

"Good night, little ghosts," Angie said with a smile;
"there's an empty house to haunt, down the street about a mile."
And the ghosts disappeared right into thin air.
She looked and she listened, but nothing was there.

She checked under her bed and behind the door.
"They're gone," whispered Angie, "there are no more."
It seemed that Jazz had been right all along;
those creatures just needed a place to belong.

But Angie's room was not the place
for creepy crawlers or a scary face.
So she said good-bye to her friends, finding homes for them all,
and did like Jazz and curled up in a ball.

Note to Parents and Teachers

The DreamDog series is about child empowerment, children learning that they have the power to solve many of their own problems while building self-confidence and happiness... with a little help from a magic dog and her rainbow tail! In the series, Jazz guides children to find the answers within themselves.

Life Lessons for All Ages

Each of the DreamDog books explores a different life lesson -- valuable lessons for any age. The first book, *Monsters in Your Bed... Monsters in Your Head*, deals with fear. Fear is often a natural consequence of growing up, of children learning about themselves, others, and their world. As parents and teachers, we can help children by providing a safe environment where their fears can be discussed. Sometimes, if these feelings of anxiety can't be expressed in real-life terms, they may surface in many ways, such as fear of the dark, or perhaps imaginary creatures. This book creates an opportunity for children to voice those fears.

The DreamDog Experience

The DreamDog series encourages children to feel secure so they will be able to share their feelings -- even the ones they perceive as being negative. By truly listening, Jazz communicates that what Angie says is of value, and that her feelings have worth. The fact that Angie sees monsters in her bed while Jazz knows they're just in her head isn't important. What matters is that Jazz "sees" Angie's reality. As parents, we can instill confidence and self-esteem by listening to our children and acknowledging their reality. Hopefully, the book will encourage you and your children to talk about and find solutions for their fears.

Open a Dialogue with Your Children

Using this book, you can open a dialogue with your children, and together you can think of your own creative solutions to help them deal with their fears. Jazz offers Angie the idea of saying "good-bye" to her fears... releasing them, letting go. We can support our children in saying "good-bye" just by being with them and listening. When Angie says good-bye to all her fears at once, nothing happens. Jazz explains that she has to address them by name -- face her fears one at a time, then she can truly let go. When Angie takes action and finds her own solution, we see an empowered, happy child -- peacefully sleeping now that she has put her fears to bed. That's the DreamDog difference... enabling children to see how strong they are, all on their own.

Explore Educational Activities

DreamDog books will appeal to children of all ages, targeting different lessons for them to learn. The youngest readers/listeners can use the book to learn colors and numbers. It's easy to teach colors using the "monsters of purple and blue... the yellow bats with spots of green... the caterpillars of orange and red," and all the rest of the cast of colorful characters. Or, children can learn or practice their numbers by counting the characters on each page, then adding and subtracting as they come and go. Older children will understand the importance of the life lessons offered in the book and can use those ideas as stepping stones to create their own solutions. They can even make up stories about the magical characters and what happens to them in their new homes. These are just a few of the many ways you and your children/students can enjoy this book.

Find the Heart

Finally, there's a fun to-do activity... find the heart! On each page, there is a hidden heart. Jazz teaches that when we take care of ourselves and others, our hearts are full. This may be a good opportunity to explain the plight of homelessness to your children and that by buying this book they have made a contribution to organizations that help homeless children. You can start the conversation by talking about how the monsters used Angie's room as their "temporary shelter" until she was able to help them each find a home of their own. Jazz the DreamDog will encourage your children to try to understand others... she'll help them find the heart!

Let us know what you think! Please share your experiences by visiting us at www.dreamdog.com